THE DANDY

£6.99

Printed and Published in Great Britain by
D. C. THOMSON & CO. LTD.,
185 Fleet Street, London, EC4A 2HS
© D. C. THOMSON & CO., LTD., 2005
ISBN 1 84535 041 3

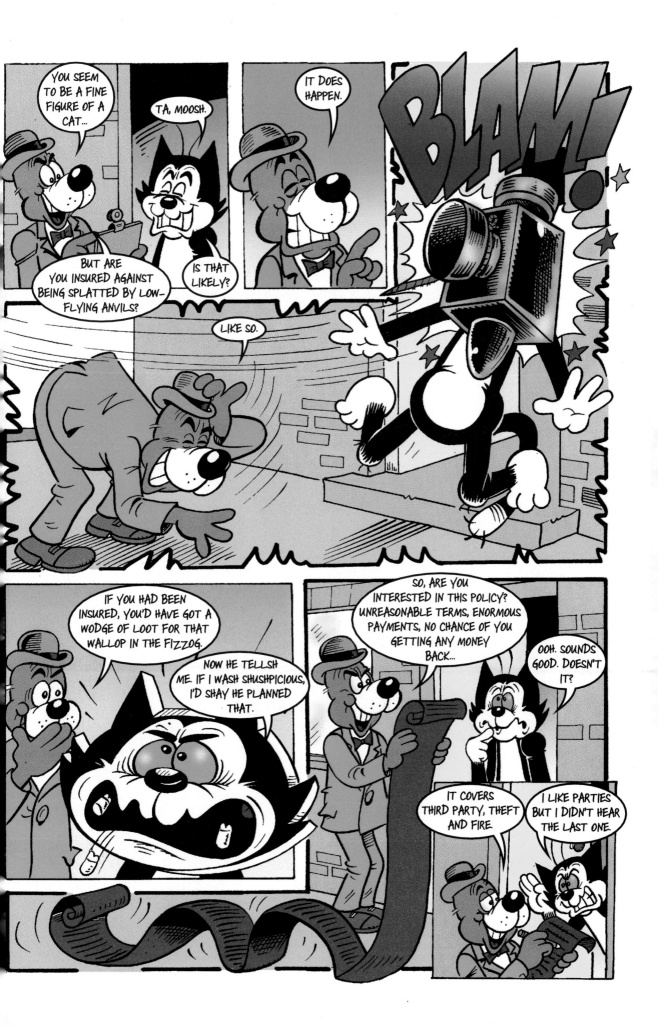

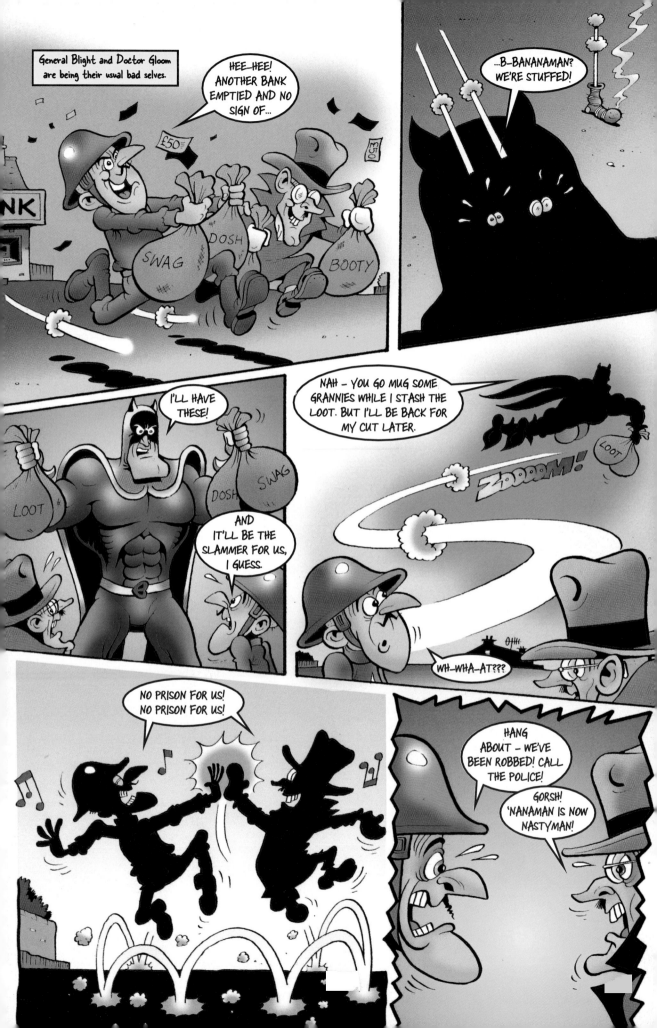

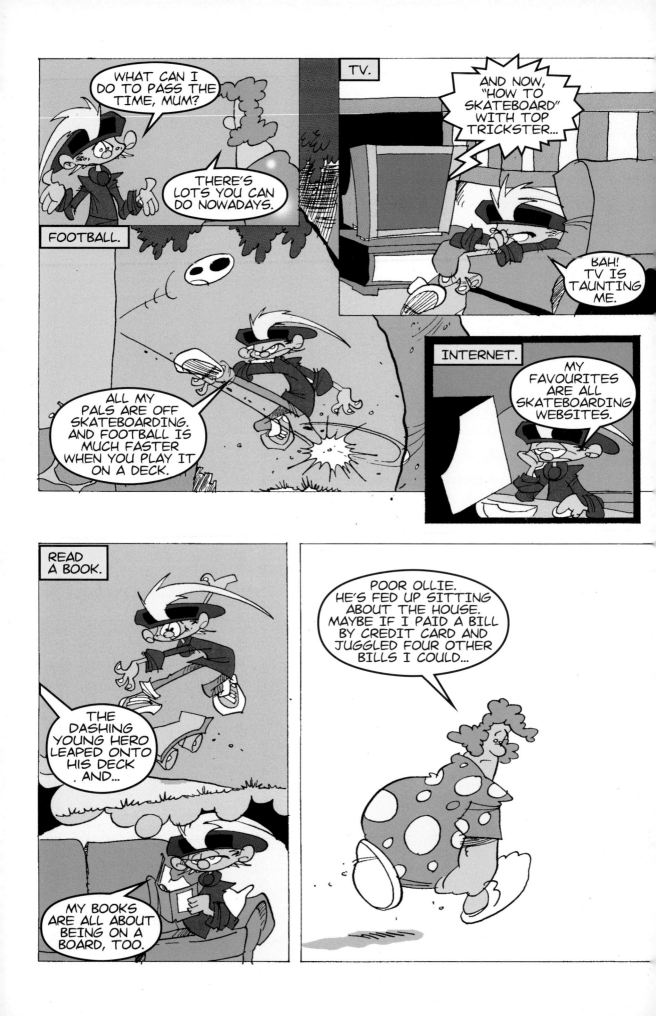

BERYL THE PERIL

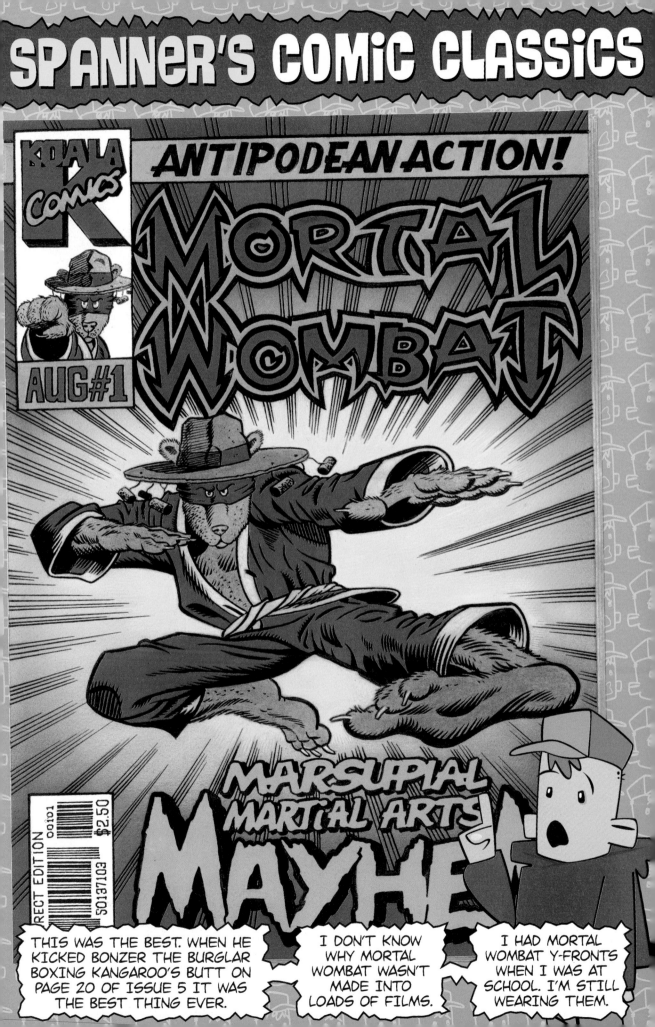

KOALA Comics

AUG #1

ANTIPODEAN ACTION!

MORTAL WOMBAT

MARSUPIAL MARTIAL ARTS MAYHEM

RECT EDITION 00101 $2.50

S0137103

THIS WAS THE BEST. WHEN HE KICKED BONZER THE BURGLAR BOXING KANGAROO'S BUTT ON PAGE 20 OF ISSUE 5 IT WAS THE BEST THING EVER.

I DON'T KNOW WHY MORTAL WOMBAT WASN'T MADE INTO LOADS OF FILMS.

I HAD MORTAL WOMBAT Y-FRONTS WHEN I WAS AT SCHOOL. I'M STILL WEARING THEM.

Q: WHAT'S GREEN AND RUNS AROUND THE GARDEN?
A: A HEDGE!

Q: WHAT SWEETS DO ALIENS EAT?
A: MARTIAN MALLOWS!

Q: WHAT TESTS DO WIZARDS DO AT SCHOOL?
A: SPELLING!

Q: DID YOU HEAR ABOUT THE ROBBER WHO FELL INTO A CEMENT MIXER?
A: HE WAS A HARDENED CRIMINAL!

Q: WHAT KIND OF BIRD OPENS DOORS?
A: A KIWI!

Q: WHAT GAME DO VAMPIRES PLAY?
A: CASKETBALL!

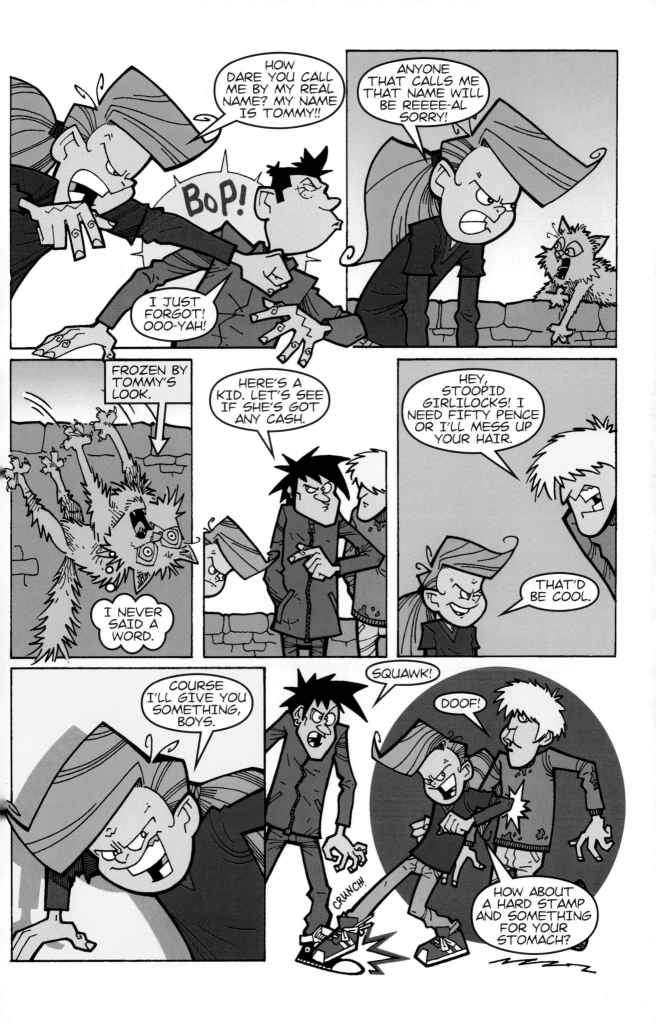

MARBLE COMICS

NOT APPROVED BY THE COMICS CODE AUTHORITY

HE'S HEROIC! HE'S HAIRY! HE'S

HAMSTERMAN
-RODENT AVENGER

MARBLE COMICS GROUP

NO.1 JUNE

10¢

T LURKS WITHIN THE

HAMSTERMAN WAS THE BEST COMIC OF THE 1960s. FACT!

THERE SHOULD HAVE BEEN A HAMSTERMAN FILM - WITH CLINT EASTWOOD AS HAMSTERMAN.

I SPENT AGES LOOKING FOR THIS IN THE COMIC SHOP UNTIL I FOUND IT BEHIND A RADIATOR BUNGING UP A LEAK. THE COMIC SHOP GUY DOESN'T KNOW CLASS WHEN HE SEES IT.

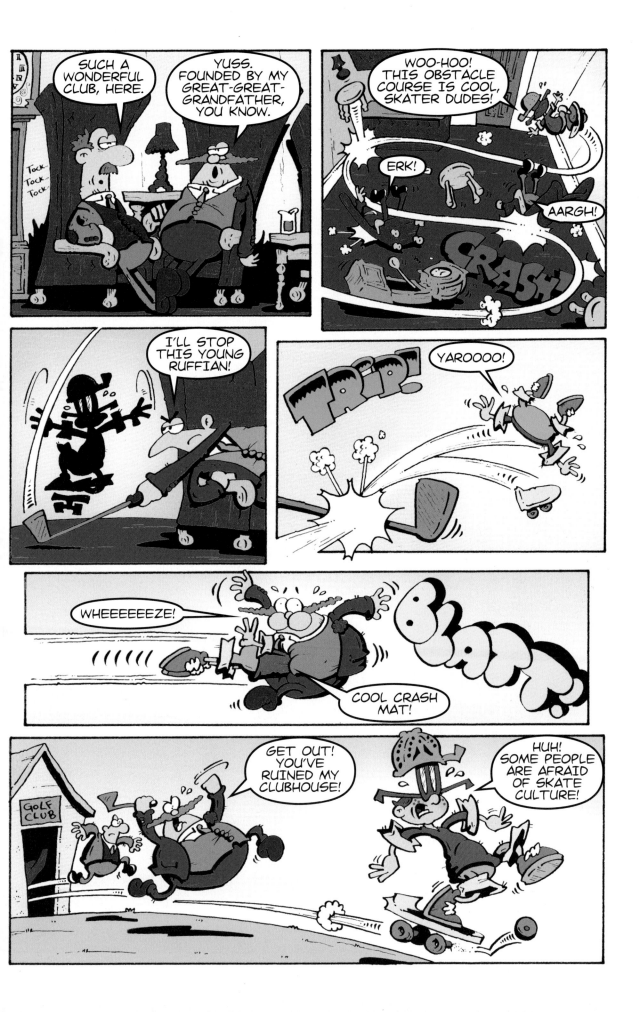

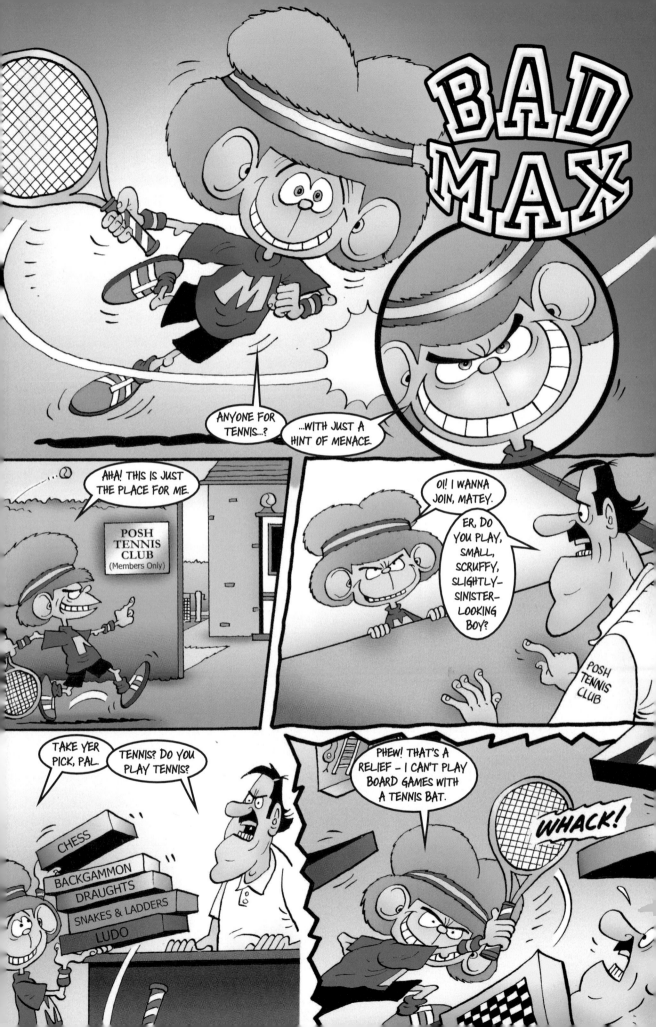

STEVE BRIGHT

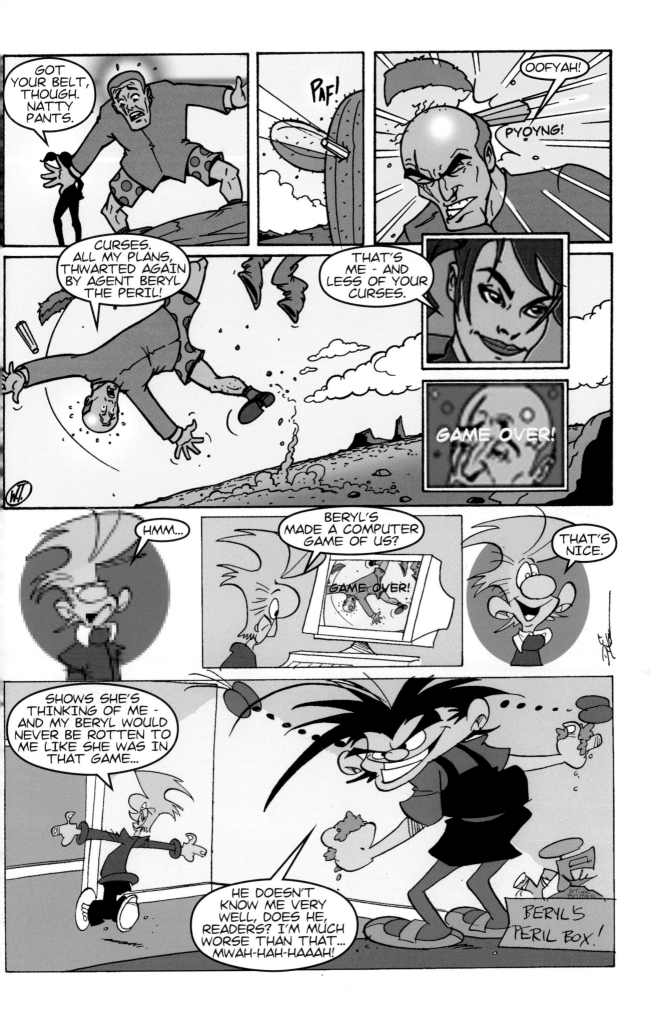

TYPE 'O'
COMICS

1
OCT 04

US $2-50
UK£1-50

the
bottom
Vampire

GPM'04

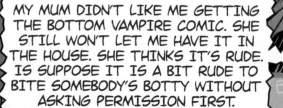

MY MUM DIDN'T LIKE ME GETTING THE BOTTOM VAMPIRE COMIC. SHE STILL WON'T LET ME HAVE IT IN THE HOUSE. SHE THINKS IT'S RUDE. I SUPPOSE IT IS A BIT RUDE TO BITE SOMEBODY'S BOTTY WITHOUT ASKING PERMISSION FIRST.

I ALWAYS EAT GARLIC AFTER I READ THIS COMIC.

IF YOU ROLL UP A COPY OF THE BOTTOM VAMPIRE COMIC YOU CAN PRETEND TO USE IT AS A STAKE. IT DOESN'T WORK ON REAL VAMPIRES THOUGH. THEY'RE NOT ALLERGIC TO PAPER.

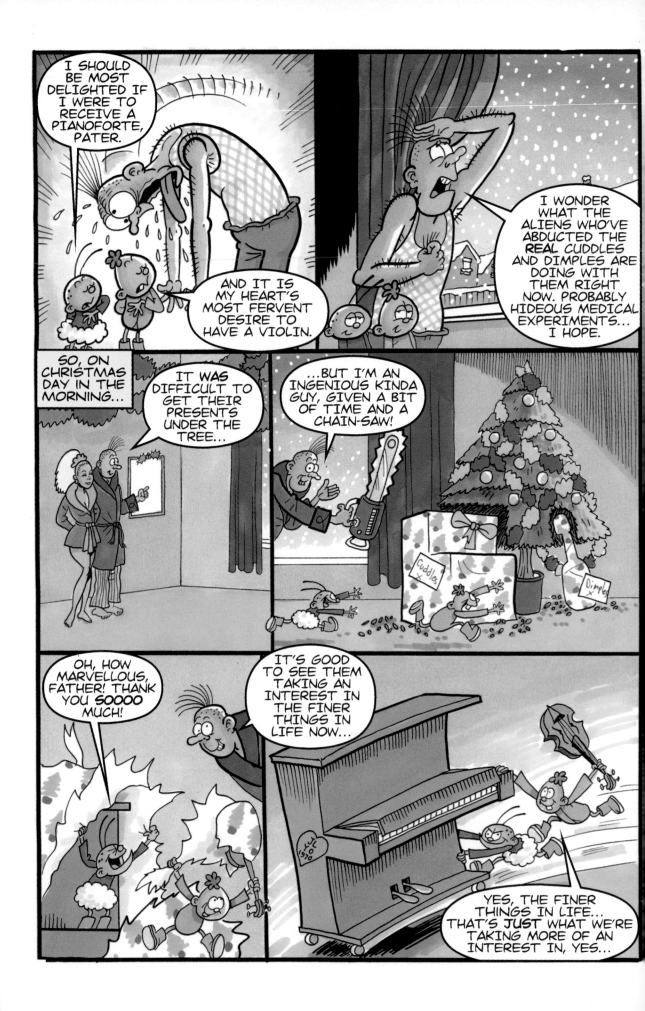

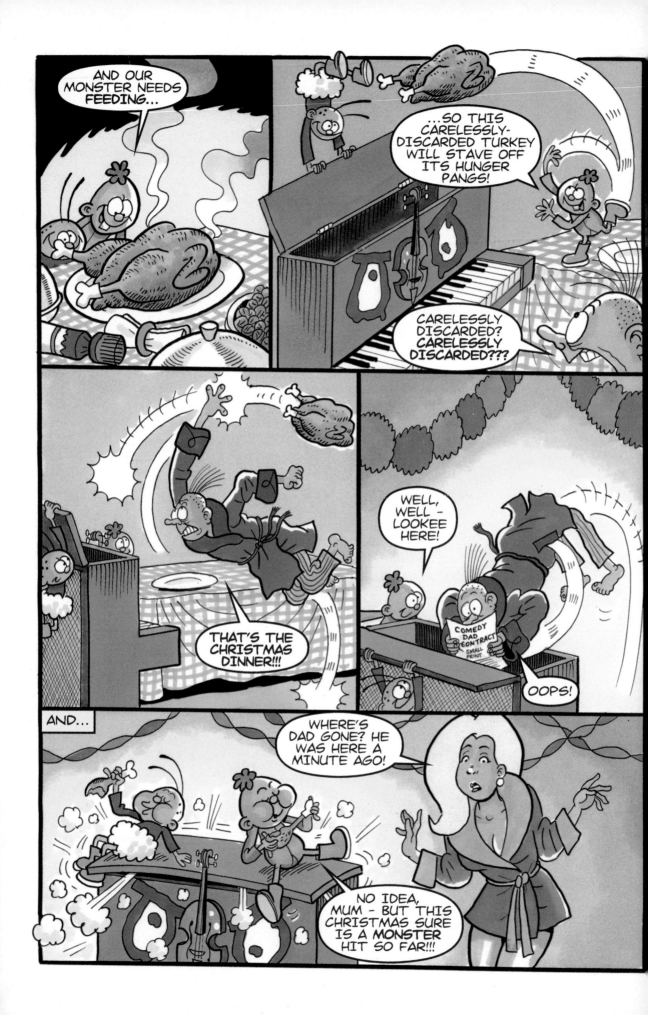

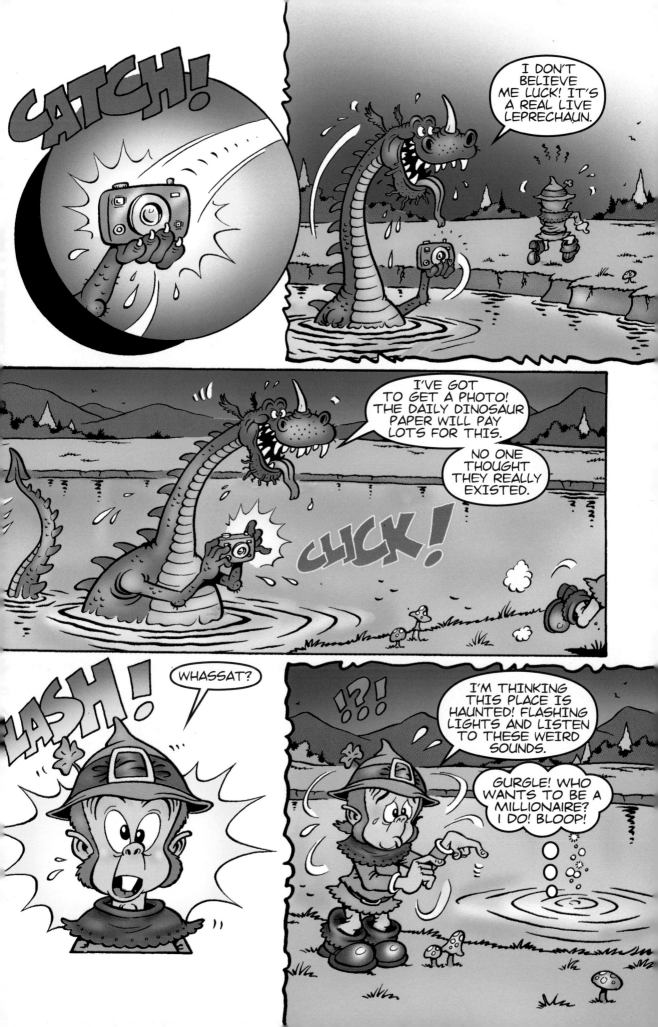